God

Left

Town

on

a

Tuesday

GOD LEFT TOWN ON A TUESDAY

the ravings of a creator gone psycho

a totally-cosmic fable

by d.v. robbins

Raven House, L.L.C.
1201 Waterfront Drive, 301
Virginia Beach, VA   23451-6454
Phone/Fax: 757-491-8356
e-mail: RavenHse@aol.com

Raven House, L.L.C.
1201 Waterfront Drive, 301
Virginia Beach, VA   23451-6454

Publisher's Cataloging-in-Publication Data
        (Prepared by Quality Books, Inc.)

robbins, d. v., 1946-
    God Left Town on a Tuesday : the ravings of a Creator gone psycho : a totally-cosmic fable / by d. v. robbins.
    p.cm.
    ISBN 0-9644907-4-9

    I. Title

PS3568.033G64 1996   813'.54
                                        QBI96-40668

Printed in the United States of America

10 9 8 7 6 5 4 3 2 1

Edited by Rebecca Al Bramer and Mary Ann Anderson
Illustrations by Jeff Fitzgerald

DEDICATION

For Violet and Laurence,

and for Tim.

Wish you were here.

CONTENTS

ILLUSTRATIONS

<u>**Introduction**</u>

It was a dark and stormy night.

No, no, no. Not hardly.

It was a miserably hot and windy day. Or maybe it was a cold and snowy afternoon, with freezing ice and sleet.

Who cares?

The point is, I was sitting at the kitchen table with a stack of unpaid bills in front of me, moaning and groaning about my miserable, pathetic life. I wanted to know what was going on, and why me?

Suddenly, Dionne Warwick singing ***What's it all about, Alfie,*** came blaring from my radio . . . a song whose lyrics SEARCH FOR AN ANSWER to life's most complex and frustrating problems. What made it even more intriguing was the fact my radio had been tuned to 96X, a station that caters to the boisterous, "Why don't you just kill me?" crowd. I don't normally patronize this particular breed of noise, however, on "I can't pay my bills" day, it somehow seemed appropriate.

The point is, 96X does not play theme music. NOT EVER.

Add it all up, folks. We're talking Cosmic Moment. You've got to acknowledge the Dionne Warwick Connection. The Psychic Friend's Hotline . . . hmmm? Oh yeah. She and her people were reaching out.

There was something happening here. Something mystical and serendipitous. *Someone was toying with my brain.*

Okay, I listened. Tra-la-la-la.

I sucked in the words, trying feverishly to make a paranormal association. What was Dionne trying to tell me?

I got nothing.

All of a sudden, just as I was about to dismiss the 96X-thing as a freakish quirk of nature, maybe a surge from magnetic power lines, my hand started to move involuntarily across the table. A cheap, drugstore pen began to scrawl words, then sentences, all over my phone bill. Automatic writing. Instructions from "Beyond The Veil."

I'm a liar. None of what you just read is true.

As I recall, the television was on. Right in the middle of "The People's Court," a big head appeared, taking up most of the screen. Yeah, that's what happened. The huge head talked to me in a hypnotic drone and I felt myself slip away . . . far, far away. My bills became an insignificant pile of waste . . .

I was channeling God. He wanted me to deliver His message by writing this book.

Oh, please. I'm making myself sick. I had a conversation with God, all right. I did most of the talking. If memory serves me correctly, I was pulling a wad of bubble gum out of The Christ Child's nose . . . a life size nativity scene having been a target for some local pranksters. I acknowledged this was a rather benign practical joke, but irreverent just the same. I told God, if I were Him, I'd be on the next train out of town. The gum-in-the-nose-thing was merely the tip of the iceberg. Why hang around and watch the entire human race self-destruct?

That was *my* suggestion, for what it was worth.

I could NOT believe my ears. He agreed with me, leaving town was an excellent idea. Tuesday was good for Him. Enough said. He signed off and went home to pack.

He didn't sign off for long. The Man went psycho; started yelling and screaming and giving us all "what-for." You must have heard Him, how could you have not?

In case you missed it . . . maybe that was the day you had root canal surgery and were zoned out on nitrous oxide . . . an encore presentation has been reconstructed for your convenience. Of course, it's not the same as "being there."

He was pretty ticked-off. You should really check it out.

You might regret it if you don't.

I cleared a path in all directions,
so you might choose your journey,

I lit up the night with a million stars
to help you find your way.

I offered My hand, as the walk is sometimes lonely.

Then, of course, I promised you Eternity.

You are definitely going to miss Me when I'm gone.

G.

<u>**Chapter One**</u>

"Oh Lord, won't you buy me a Mercedes Benz,
My friends all drive Porsches, I must make amends . . .
Worked hard all my lifetime
No help from my friends,
Oh Lord, won't you buy me a Mercedes Benz?"
Janis Joplin

Sure thing. Right after I buy you a house on the ocean and a ten carat solitaire from Harry Winston's. Who do I look like, John D. Rockefeller? Oy.

* * * * *

Now you've done it.

You've pushed Me over the edge.

Come next Tuesday . . .

I'll be on the last train out of town, headed for parts unknown.

I won't be looking back and there is nothing you can do to change My mind.

I know what you're thinking. You're thinking, "He's just mad."

Dagblasted straight I am, pardon My French. I have half a mind to take your gravity away!

Does this look like My "Happy Face?"

Ha! Not that it matters. Oh, you'd be shook up for a moment or two, all teary eyed and apologetic. It's the old "we promise we won't do it again" routine. The whole time you'd be looking down at your watches, just hankering to get to your "Dukes of Hazzard" re-runs. Remember this, however: There's not too much TV watching that could go on without gravity.

I know, I know. I've threatened to leave a million times before, but this time I mean it. I'm packing, as we speak. Actually, it feels kind of good. No more, "Dear God, I'd like a Sony Trinitron with a picture-in-a-picture" or "I could really use an IBM Think Pad-365 series, with 8 MB RAM, 540 MB hard drive and an Intel DX4 75 MHz processor." Not to mention the "Reebok Pump." And Nintendo. What happened to good old leather sandals . . . comfortable, affordable, and pleasing to the eye? When did kick-the-can and hopscotch become obsolete? I turn My head for barely a cosmic moment and the next thing I know, you need a joy stick and a Ph.D. from Harvard to play a game.

I'm looking forward to not spending the better part of an evening listening to Charlotte DeBerg from Swiftwater Idaho ask Me if I would please give her Walter Slotnik. I'm not running a dating service up here. It would be different if she asked for some tips on how to get Walter Slotnik herself. I'm very tired of being expected to do all the work, all the time. It's wearing Me out.

Never mind the begging. It's too late for that. I've talked the talk, now I'm walking the walk. Adios, My oblivious Jugheads. See what it's REALLY like without Me.

Are you serious? You can sit there with a straight face and ask Me why? As if you don't know! I was here before wind and rain. Before yesterday and tomorrow were even born.

I have heard the sweet laughter of mermaids.

I have danced with Aphrodite.

I have seen the Phoenix rise.

I've been around the block a million times and I know your tricks.

You are trying to stall for time . . . a technique that, unfortunately, worked with limited success in the past.

Like when? Like WHEN??

Like back around 2000 BC when you insisted on nailing the hides of your enemies in various spots around town for public viewing, after a rather painful fillet-job, I might add. I WAS NOT amused. It's bad enough you have always considered animal heads, hides, hooves and horns to be appropriate decorating accessories. I draw the line at human wall hangings. Anyway, it seemed you were liking this a little too much, and I was just about to blast you with a very nasty-yet-effective global drought, when some of you saw the warning signs. Oh, you promised to be good. You'd change, you'd get your act together.

I caved in, is what I did. I took you at your word. The next thing I knew, you were feeding each other to the lions.

Sometimes I think, "If only I hadn't let them invent the AK-47 Assault Rifle." Then I quickly realize there would only be more of you pushing each other in front of moving trains.

In any event, there will be no stalling for time. I am checking out of here for once and for all. The only regret I have is that I didn't do it sooner.

<u>**Chapter Two**</u>

Do you think I could PLEASE pack in peace? Blah, blah, blah. "You can't help yourselves. You know not what you do."

Cut Me a break. You know EXACTLY "what you do." You pester. You whine. You "gimmee, gimmee, gimmee." You're suffering from PMS, attention deficit disorder, mid-life crisis, repressed memory syndrome, post traumatic stress, inner city rage, and you're depraved on account of you're deprived. Demons talk to you while you sleep and tell you to rob the closest Seven-Eleven with a sawed-off shotgun.

Then you have the unmitigated gall to patronize Me with the "Let's Make A Deal" routine. I scratch your back and you'll scratch Mine. How many times have I been sucked into that one?

Frankly, I don't mind the empty promises. For the most part, it keeps you humble.

I'm not Monty Hall, however, and I'm out of the deal-making business. I've been burned too many times.

Here is the *most amazing thing.*

Sometimes I sit up here listening to you ramble on and on for hours: you're having a hard time choosing between a Lexus and an Acura, whatever. On occasion, you might even THANK ME for certain aspects of your life.   Suddenly, it will occur to Me you are merely

PERFORMING! You aren't even sure I exist! What you're doing is covering yourself, just in case *I really am "out there!"*

Do you know what it makes Me feel like to know our relationship is based on fear? DO YOU? It hurts! It's very condescending. What makes it worse is you think I don't know the difference!

Here is an expansion of that thought.

I could simply tell you *I am,* or . . .

I could straddle the Hudson River draped in a gold lamé shroud, with bolts of lightning shooting from My fingertips. To make sure I had your attention, I'd sing several choruses from a nice show tune, maybe from *Cats* or *La Cage aux Folle.* Then, I'd break-dance in Macy's window, as a kicker.

Some of you would believe it for about ten seconds, then write it off as a hi-tech laser show. Others would believe it forever, *but these folks were believers to begin with.*

Most of you would think I was an alien being, demonstrating My superiority. You would run screaming into the night, expecting Me to take your blood and conduct experiments on your children. Of course, this is the same group of people who think Elvis is alive and writing country and western music under the name of Ricky-Raye Travis, Jr.

You don't want documented proof that I exist, as much as you complain I never offer you any .

I have been so close, you have heard the quickness of My breath.

How many times have I whispered your name . . .
a million times, maybe more.

I have shown you repeatedly that I AM.
When will you hear Me? Now, as I pack to leave?

You'd rather moan and groan to The Myth, just like you're doing right this very moment.

I am not being cruel and *unGod-like* . . . definitely NOT.

I am merely talking to you the way you talk to Me. How does it feel?

Enough already! I don't have to explain myself. Nor do I have the desire to wile away these last few hours with this rather pointless conversation; *YOU* pretending to be shocked, confused, and totally in the dark over My decision to split, interspersed with an occasional outburst from Me. I don't NEED the aggravation!

Aye-yi-yi.

Okay, okay. Because I am a fair and judicious God, I will allow Myself to be swayed ever so slightly. Once again, I will assume you *REALLY DON'T GET IT*. Furthermore, I don't want to be riddled with guilt once I'm on the road . . . picturing your faces all twisted into pitiful frowns, drooping with that "what-happened?" look. (I can't believe I'm doing this. I swore I would never get sucked in again. Suddenly, I am feeling very "wus-like.")

Here it is. Here's the straw that broke the camels back . . .

Your obsession with political correctness is slowly, but surely, destroying My image, My persona.

Since the beginning of time I have been
> *Allah,*
> *Jeshua,*
> *Jehovah.*

I am the solemn eyes of the Great Sphinx.

The many faces on the totem pole.

I am also The Man in The White Robe, with soft and gentle eyes, *because that is what you asked Me to be.* Commanded Me to be.

Suddenly, there is an uneasiness growing among you. I am no longer any of these things . . . I am amorphous.

"Oh, really?" you say. "That's because we made a mistake. A REAL GOD would not want to assume a specific gender and stature. An honest God would want to be a generic, androgynous being with no particular persuasion, like a snail or an earthworm. A fair God would not mind being overhauled.. You know, so as not to offend anybody."

OFFEND?!

Since when is assuming the role of Universal Patriarch offensive? Especially when it was YOUR IDEA?

So many lifetimes ago, you gave Me an identity, and now you want to change it. Take it away. You are proud of yourself, succumbing to the overly sensitive egos of the politically correct. You call it justice.

I call it *"Mydiuti Fofyyedd."* I won't bother translating that for you. Use your imagination.

Altering the Image of God. I've never worn a dress before.

Maybe, to keep within the parameters of fine family values, you can re-paint the Sistine Chapel. Present Me to the World surrounded by My newly acquired family: 2.5 children; a nice, attractive wife who stays at home, yet is her "own person." A dog, maybe a collie or Labrador retriever. A Labrador retriever, however, is not politically correct because this is an animal which has been bred to hunt, and hunting surely is a no-no. So, let's go with the collie. A vegetarian collie.

Behind Me, as a backdrop, there could be God's New Home: a house made of . . . old, recycled soda bottles and laundry detergent containers. I shall buzz around Heaven on a red scooter, a non-polluting vehicle which will also give Me the exercise needed to maintain proper health.

Why is THAT so outlandish, when you have already seen fit to change My Words?

"Our Mother/Father, who art in Heaven."

The next thing you know, you'll have transformed Santa Claus into a genderless "it."

You could go with "Saint Nicholas/Nicole, a right jolly old elf/elfette."

You're actually thinking about this, aren't you?

You must understand. I am not at all disturbed by the countless faces you have already given Me. It is the dismantling of these previously defined and established faces that is of concern. If you want to go to Times Square and build yourself a statue of a three-headed water buffalo, calling it The God Of The Open Range, go ahead. Be my guest.

You see, in essence you are handing Me a "pink slip." This is the first phase of the inevitable "reconstruction." The "downsizing." It says "You are not doing a good job."

You may think I am over-reacting; however, I know without question that this minuscule alteration is just the beginning. Soon, I will be stripped bare, molded and remolded, until I am an indefinable glob. Like a discarded collage of this and that, hanging in a forgotten corner of an attic.

Then, I will be nothing.

Well. Before that happens, to speak in a language I know you will understand, you are now about to become Creator-Deprived. How do you like THAT for political correctness?

It is this kind of absurdity which has, in the past, forced Me into compromising positions. You know, blasting you with the dreaded "Three F's." Flood, Fire and Famine. Hopefully, you can imagine how frustrated I must have been to have taken such drastic measures. It pained Me greatly. Afterward, I couldn't even look down upon you. As a matter of fact, I became *SO* depressed, I think it was after the plague of locusts, I vowed to stop reacting to your horrific behavior in that fashion.

Actually, I've become a pretty laid-back kind of guy.

Oh yes I have.

Instead of blowing My top, I've entertained a more passive approach. Like providing you with positive role models to emulate. Over and over, I send them down.

Over and over, you knock them off.

And you have the nerve to ask Me why I'm leaving. If I was The Old Me, I'd be tempted to squash you flatter than a Perry Como Record Album. (For those of you who are too young to relate to record albums OR Perry Como, think "Hootie and the Blowfish" on compact disc.) Instead, I am leaving town. The hermaphrodite-thing was the last straw.

You people need to get a life.

I am not ranting and raving!

No, I am not. Even if I were, I don't think you have any room to comment. How many nights have I sat up here listening to *YOU* go on and on in no particular direction, in many instances blaming *ME* for your miserable existence? "I'm cold, I'm hot. How am I going to pay my American Express bill? *I wish I could find a good pair of walking shoes for under a hundred dollars. WHY DON'T YOU ANSWER ME?"*

What you fail to understand is that I have nothing whatsoever to do with the choices YOU make. What do you think My role *REALLY IS*? I'll tell you, because it is painfully obvious that you haven't a clue.

I advise. I nurture. And, I LISTEN. If you were honest, you would admit that listening is what you want most, anyway! Ask any bartender! Customers unload their problems on a bartender not because he is an expert in problem solving . . . he is the consummate *listener!*

Okay, it's fair for you to ask: if I'm so thrilled to be a listener, why don't I want to hear about your migraine headaches, or your overdrawn bank account?

I do want to hear about them. I simply am unwilling to be BLAMED for them.

I will not reach down and untangle every knot.

I have given you what you need to take care of yourself.

You also must acknowledge there are things in this world which are out of your control. You must NOT, however, use these inevitabilities as an excuse to commit atrocities upon each other, or BLAME ME with the old "It must be God's will."

Believe it or not, I have better things to do with My time than to curse you with heart attacks and terminal diseases or arrange for you to lose your job to an illegal alien.

Besides . . . who ever promised you a rose garden?

You'd like to make Me the scapegoat for all misfortune. It's easier that way.

It's not getting any better. I'm leaving town on Tuesday and you cannot stop Me.

Please give Me some privacy, as I cannot think through all the chatter and commotion.

I shall not be moved.

Chapter Three

Okay . . . so I'll be moved a little.

It's obvious I cannot shake you. I understand the last-ditch effort.
Everything goes. No holds barred. Try everything and anything.

You think you have nothing to lose.

Go ahead and blabber away. I certainly can talk and pack at the same
time.

Not that I want to. I feel as if I've talked Myself blue in the face over
the course of several thousand eons. You never listen until I'm ready
to blow a head gasket.

So, what's your point?

Oh, I get it. You see me putting My things in a suitcase and it occurs to you that I really am hitting the road. Now you are pretending to **ACCEPT** My departure, but it would be great if I would counsel you a bit and prepare you for what lies ahead. Suddenly, you are more than willing to have your indiscretions laid out before you.

Hmmm.

Different, yet effective. (Don't gloat. This is **NOT** a concession. This is idle chatter designed to pass the time while I pack. That's all, nothing more.)

First of all, you must know that most of your problems stem from the fact that there are just **TOO MANY** people! I've got to say, you folks gave new meaning to the "go forth and multiply" thing. There's no stopping you! You're stacked on top of each other like crates in a Japanese warehouse. Is it any wonder that you're impatient, frustrated and easily agitated?

Didn't it ever occur to you that there might be a good reason **WHY** childbirth is so painful? Nature is talking to you . . . She is saying, "This is a wonderful, miraculous moment, but please jot this down . . . **IT HURTS!**" After slamming your hand in the car door, would you wait a week, then do it again?

I am saddened by the numbers of unwanted children. There are too many.

I suppose, when all is said and done, *I COULD HAVE* tinkered with the evolutionary process and made childbirth a bit easier and less painful. A wider birth canal, maybe.

Believe Me. There would be less name-calling in the delivery room, a place where no man is safe from a scathing tongue. My name comes up often, and not in a way I am willing to repeat.

Fortunately, I am a tolerant and loving Creator who puts things in proper perspective. I forgive the attack on Me because, as I said, in many respects I feel responsible for the way the human anatomy evolved.

I have strayed from the point. The bottom line is, you have to find something else to do with your time. Read a book, mow the lawn. Clean up the Long Island Expressway, it's a dumpster, for Pete's sake.

I guess what I'm trying to say is that you must learn to practice moderation. Don't take everything you do to such an extreme! You are a civilization of "shockers." Shock, shock, shock!

Ah! Green spiked hair, for instance. I am completely aware that this particular display is merely a metaphor for something which goes far beyond that which meets the eye. Beneath the jungle of frozen quill and spur, lurks a relevant social statement. "Damn the establishment," or something on that order.

What it says to Me is, " Duh, I've stuck a fork in an electrical outlet."

I've stuck a fork in the electrical outlet.

I AM NOT MAKING FUN OF YOU! I am simply pointing out some of the outlandish ways you look for attention.

Then, of course, you resent the attention once you've gotten it.

Let's see.

Music that is more noise than melody. Snappy little tunes like, "Life Stinks Bad and So Do You," by R. B. Ice Pick.

> "Cross my heart, hope to die
> Stick a steak knife in my eye
>
> Slap me, punch me
> Shoot me dead,
>
> Jab a meat hook through my head . . .
>
> Burn my carcass, when you're through,
> 'cause Life Stinks Bad and so do you."

Why don't you stand behind Me and rub two Styrofoam cooler lids together?

There you go, getting all paranoid and overly sensitive. It just so happens I never cared much for the "fugue and baroque" era, either. So morose and tiresome. Ho-hum, I'm falling asleep just thinking about it. I don't know where such a boring generation of people came from.

Bagpipes make the hairs on the back of My neck stand at attention.

"Who put the bop in the bob-sh-bop-sh-bop, who put the dip in the dip-sh-dip-sh-dip . . ." I don't get *that* at all.

The point is, and I've said this before, I'm not moved to tears by everything you do!

Just for future reference, here's something *I DO* like. I like a nice piano piece, *Autumn Leaves*, or something on that order. The musician does not jump up from the piano after playing *Autumn Leaves* and set himself on fire. Nor does he bite the tail off a hamster, then spew it into the audience. This is good.

I'm sorry, but *YOU* asked for My opinion. I wanted to be left alone to pack, but you *HAD* to interfere. Now you're disturbed by what I have to say.

I should have known better!

Here's an analogy I know you can relate to.

It's like the woman who has just zipped her size 16 body into a size 7 leather skirt, asking her husband if she looks fat.

There is no good answer.

Honesty gets him a night on the couch. A lie forces him to spend the evening parading around the mall with a woman who thinks she is Cher.

Equal time for the gender-sensitive.

A middle-aged man going through mid-life crisis asks his wife if she thinks he is going bald.

"No dear. Your hair is as thick as the day I met you. "

Or . . .

"Yes dear. Get out of the sun, the bounce-back is burning out my corneas."

Again, it's a no win situation. A "yes" answer assures her the UPS man will be at the door by the end of the week with a ten gallon jug of Rogaine. A "no" answer condemns her to a lifetime of "the hair-drape."

I will not be pinned against a wall, my dear children. I am going to be honest and forthright. I have nothing to lose!

You're analyzing every word I'm saying, looking for an excuse to be offended . . .

So sue Me. (I mean that in the most figurative sense; however, I can see the wheels turning. It would be The Ultimate Lawsuit, wouldn't it now? Me, against you and the Dream Team.)

I care not! Come next Tuesday, I'll be on the road to extinction, right up there with the woolly mammoth and the dodo bird.

Okay, let's get back on track.

> * Don't shave a poodle down to its bare skin. Those
> balls of fur around its ankles and the frizzy tuft on top of
> its head look ridiculous. Furthermore, the dog is the

laughing stock of the neighborhood. Let the animal live with dignity and respect.

* Don't pick names for your children out of books on Animal Husbandry or Farm Equipment Catalogues.

Drake, Stallion, Steed.
Silo, Thresher, Deere.

In twenty years, the child you named "Serendipity" or "Magnum" will be on the talk show circuit, telling the world about how the only job he or she can get is being a body double for the cast of *Baywatch*.

Now that I have you standing at attention, I simply must mention a curiosity that has bewildered Me for the longest time. There must be something going on which is so profound and deep that somehow I have missed the point. If you are still speaking to Me (It has become fairly obvious you suddenly have very little to say. Cat got your tongue?), I would like you to explain the following:

* A Mary and Joseph salt and pepper shaker. Are condiments meant to be a "religious experience"?

* The Blessed Mother Air freshener. In the bathroom, on top of the commode?

* Jesus on velvet. Not even GOOD velvet. Very BAD velvet that can hardly withstand the blistering heat of gas station tarmac for an entire weekend.

* The Head-Of-Christ-Piggy-Bank, with a coin slot chiseled into His skull, midst the crown of thorns. Hell-o-o! I am NOT IMPRESSED!

* Jesus behind Plexiglas, with eyes that blink, blink, blink (depending on where you're standing). THIS is a very scary item. Children see it and go running.

* Bathtub Mary. (For the very few of you who have never witnessed such a sight, Bathtub Mary is a shrine dedicated to the Virgin Mother, made from an old bathtub. It is buried on end - let's say up to the soap dish - in a garden, or used to hide a cement well cover. Mary is IN THE TUB, protected from the elements by the sanctuary of discarded plumbing.)

* The Holy Family wall clock. The three of Them, embedded in walnut, then shellacked slicker than the toes of Bojangles' tap shoes. (No ethnic slur intended.) Six O'clock is an amusing sight.

* The Last Supper Beach Towel. Very bad. *Very, very bad.*

The Irreverent Bumper Sticker Collection:

      1. BUCKLE UP FOR JESUS
      2. JESUS IS MY CO-PILOT
      3. JESUS . . . DON'T LEAVE HOME WITHOUT HIM
      4. HONK IF YOU LOVE JESUS

I asked Jesus, by the way, what He thought of that. He said he wasn't all that thrilled with having His name hanging just above an exhaust pipe. Furthermore, He didn't see much honor and respect in "horn honking" . . .

    * Sitting at an intersection.

    * Seeing the Honk for Jesus bumper sticker on the car ahead.

    * Honking like crazy, ***HONK, HONK, HONK***!!

      I don't think so.

You honk if you love square dancing.
You honk if you love Doberman pinschers.
You honk if you love Elvis.

You ***do not*** honk for The King of the Jews.

It is in **VERY BAD** taste.

You hardly **EVER** see a "Buckle up for Allah," or "Buddha On Board" bumper sticker.

I am not being sarcastic and flippant.

All right, I am.

You do things that are far more disturbing than giving your poodle a bad hair cut or wiping down with a Last Supper Beach Towel. If the worse thing you did was honk for Jesus, I wouldn't be packing My long underwear.

At this point, I won't be opening up *THAT* can of worms. No sirree.

It's too painful to discuss, not to mention the time it would take to even scratch the surface.

Okay, I can't stand to hear you whine.

Ultimate fighting, ethnic cleansing . . . TERRORISM??

Ultimate Fighting.
No biting or eye gouging allowed.

האם אתם משוגעים   (Are you people *NUTS*?)

Not that I should even have to direct your attention toward this issue. Certainly you know better than to murder each other in cold blood.

Ha! What am I thinking?? I had to hand deliver tablets of stone, not once but TWICE, in My own writing, LISTING ten common sense rules for you to follow. Don't murder, don't steal, have respect for each other . . .

If you can't remember and respect ten simple and obvious rules, why do you feel obliged to fill libraries with millions of pages of law? You can't follow the few simple instructions I gave you, yet you expect to understand and be guided by the federal tax code?

Why should I have to remind you that planting an explosive in a subway station is not a nice thing to do? As if I should have to say, "Don't do that! You'll kill and maim hundreds of innocent people!"

Sometimes I don't know what was going through My mind, way back then. I was so convinced all you needed was a little help. A nudge or two.

Maybe I interfered a little too much.

Not any more. I'll stay out of it. It's just too much trouble, always bailing you out.

And frustrating, because there is simply no learning from your mistakes.

Now, if you would **KINDLY** go away. I'm not in the mood to talk about this anymore.

<u>**Chapter Four**</u>

You are still here. My obedient servants.

Facetious, you say? You are not amused by My sense of humor?

For your information, I can be very "Comedy-Central-Funny."

Oh, yes I can.

How can you say that? ***HOW***??

Okay, just picture in your mind a Chevy Chevette, tooling down the interstate, hiked up to the Heavens on huge monster truck tires. This vehicle ***IS OUT THERE***! I see hundreds of them every day! We're talking "hilarious." You can't deny it! Could it have possibly happened without My unique wit? Who inspires you, ***hmmm***?

Or how about this little ditty I just threw together? This is REALLY FUNNY:

I am the Old Man from Forever,
Who thought it would be very clever

To allow in My plan,
A woman and man,
But it sure was a costly endeavor.

There was murder and incest and lust;
Soon all of My rules bit the dust.

It was never my goal
To lose all control,

So leaving this place is a must.

To Geraldo and Oprah and Phil:
My children just love a cheap thrill.

I've run out of luck,
and I'm passing the buck;

Take these Jugheads and do what you will.

Now, **THAT CRACKS ME UP!**

You folks need to lighten up. The world is going to be one great big chuckle, once I am gone. I almost wish I was going to be around to see it!

Just wait.   Inventions to stagger the human mind will flood the market.   A Magnetic God-Retriever, by Ronco.

patented God-retriever

How many millions will be sold, at $29.95 plus shipping and handling? Such a deal!

I can see it now. People running off to some high-energy vortex in New Mexico or Arizona, with this remarkable gadget that they bought from the shopping channel. It will be guaranteed to hunt Me down and bring Me back.

Not a chance. You will NEVER find Me. I am going to jump off the edge of the sky, a place where I'm still treated with the utmost respect.

Like you're the only thing going on around here. You wish!

I'm sorry, but it's a done deal and just talking about it makes Me want to get out of here a few days early.

Where was I?

Oh, yes.   Assuring you that I have a terrific sense of humor.   It's important you know that, because of all the bad press I've gotten over the centuries.   You know, like: *"You'd better not do that or God will strike you down with His mighty wrath."*

What does **THAT** mean, anyway? Like maybe I'll stomp on your car as you drive down the freeway, or pinch your head between My giant thumb and forefinger?

Not that I spend any appreciable amount of time yukking it up over the things you do.

I try to remain balanced. A laugh, now and then, doesn't hurt.

Warthogs, for instance.

The look, the sound . . . **what a hoot!**

Warthogs . . . what a hoot!

Whoa . . . I'm wandering.. This is supposed to be a verbal lashing, designed to **MAKE YOU THINK** about what the future holds for you, if you don't get your act together.

You will be very lonely without Me. Lonelier than you could ever imagine.

Don't grovel. It won't work this time.

Instead, get a grip on yourself and formulate a plan of action. Set some goals.

I don't know why I should care.

I DON'T CARE. I've put My last dime in the juke box. The fat lady sang loud and clear, no offense to horizontally-challenged women or the opera.

I'm singing . . .

Look, if you *REALLY* want My advice, take a short hop back to the fifties. Life was simpler and less frenetic. Of course things weren't perfect. Even then you had difficulty being nice to one another. What else is new? However, you were less inclined to drive Me nuts with selfish whining and pestering. You could live without the World Wide Web and call waiting.

Yes, you could.

YES, YOU COULD!

The thought of making Me into a morph had not yet occurred to you.

One of My favorite things about that decade . . . the bullet-nosed Studebaker. What a piece of machinery. Even though, in general, I was not that thrilled with the invention of the automobile . . . it encouraged laziness . . . this vehicle gave Me great pleasure. I spent many hours riding around with you in the back seat. Not that you ever were aware of My presence. I wouldn't have wanted to make you nervous.

Anyway, the car was doomed from the very beginning and you replaced it with Goliath monsters that sucked fuel and hogged the road. Then, after you used up all the gas, you turned to whiny little death-traps that you could bring to a stop with your foot.

I liked the Studebaker.

What a piece of machinery!

I   also like a nice mahogany desk, never caring much for the faux-wood era which really got going hot and heavy a short time later. Plastic chairs and   melmac dishes.   Fiberboard   this and that. Polyester evening wear . . . carpeting made from petroleum products.

Oh, don't stand there and tell me how you're saving the rain forest. You're talking to an Omnipotent Creator who knows all things.

Polluting the waterways with Styrofoam Cup O' Soup containers is as equally damaging to your Mother Earth. (Not that I am in favor of ravaging the wilderness and raping the forests. I will tell you once again, your basic problem is you have never practiced moderation. Everyday I watch thousands of you grab thirty or forty napkins from fast-food counters.)

Needless to say, I'm not easily impressed with man-made fibers. A nylon/rayon/dacron reasonable facsimile oriental rug will generate enough static electricity (beneath the shuffling feet of an unsuspecting victim en route to THE METAL MAGNAVOX) to jump start a Buick.

I'm into the ***"real thing!"*** Cloning, and all that genetic engineering I see going on in laboratories all over the world . . . growing babies in petrii dishes and test tubes . . . It makes Me VERY NERVOUS. I never thought I'd see the day.

Don't justify the whole thing by insinuating that if I hadn't given you the knowledge, you wouldn't have the power, therefore it's all right by Me.

IT'S NOT ALL RIGHT WITH ME.

A popular margarine commercial said it best.

> ***"It's not nice to fool Mother Nature."***

I suggest you take that advice. I really do.

It simply wasn't that long ago when children could play in their yards without having to be in view of a surveillance camera, or hooked up to an alarm system. Young mothers didn't have to walk their toddlers through a grocery store attached to a leash. Think about it . . .

How many youngsters do you see playing in vacant lots or in the street in this day and age? *Many neighborhoods seem to echo with silence, others have become a war zone.*

Computer games and cable television have become a popular way to spend time. Behind locked doors, of course.

I really miss watching children play.

Oh Fiddle-dee-dee.

Don't strain your brains thinking about what I want. (Not that you ever did.) I will be far off in the cosmosphere hanging out, trying to forget that I ever knew you.

I'm hard and cold? Ha! You should talk. Furthermore, I'd watch My mouth, if I were you. You are still the fruit of My loins and as long as you are in *My* house, you are to treat Me with respect.

What do you mean, "or what?" What kind of question is that? Or else I'll . . . confiscate every remote control on the face of the planet. The frustration will wreak global havoc, perhaps even surpassing the chaos of the Great Flood. Now, sit down and be quiet.

I'm not done.

Even if you wanted Me to, I wouldn't stop now.

I'm hot. I'm where it's at. I'm totally grooving on the moment. *I'm in "the zone."*

And . . .

Until Tuesday, I'm still The Boss.

<u>Chapter Five</u>

Now that you have all but stopped yakking completely, I'd like to initiate a philosophical discussion.

Let's, for a moment, talk "predestination."

You'd like to support this particular theory because, lo and behold, you are never held accountable for your actions! Your life becomes a pre-planned, carved-in-stone series of events for which you are helpless!

Well, think about Me, *who I am*, and the position I was in, before all of this began.

Think on this, while I tell you a story.

Is that moaning I hear? ***Tough toenails***.

One long and boring afternoon several billion years ago (To you that's a ***VERY*** long time. To me, it's a flick of a Bic.), I noticed your solar system wasn't quite in sync. There was an empty piece of real estate between Mars and Venus, just kind of "sitting there," throwing the rest of the formation off kilter.

I like things symmetrical. Always have.

Anyway, the planets were revolving and rotating . . . it was a thump-thump, thump-thumping that was happening. You know, kind of like when the steel belt in your radial tire breaks. Or when your clothes washer spins off balance.

I hate it when that happens.

I thought to Myself . . ."The black hole is okay, and sun spots are nice . . . quasars and supernovas can be a lot of fun when there's nothing else to look at . . . " I was totally bored.

I wanted to do something different with that empty space.

Something out-landish.

Something Pulitzer Prize-ish.

I wanted to be dazzled.

So, I conjured up a brew of hydrogen and carbon . . . a little bit of this and a little bit of that. I didn't know what to expect and had nothing in particular in mind . . . Okay, *THAT'S* not exactly true. I hoped *YOU* would happen, but in a spontaneous kind of way.

That's the truth.

You can go on and on with your Big Bang Theory or postulate about how I sat up here with a schematic and planned your future in precise detail . . .

Sorry. It just didn't happen that way.

No, it did not.

That would have been **SO BORING,** it would hardly have been worth the effort.

For Me, the reward was going to be in the relationship My creations and I shared. It would be a learning experience for all involved, including Me.

I must admit, giving you free will was not a wise thing to do.

It has worked both ways . . . It keeps Me out of your affairs; however, it has given you an excuse to . . .

do things to one another that are beyond even My comprehension.

The bottom line is, I whipped up a planet that supported life and it's been a day at the circus ever since.

It amazes Me that you could actually believe I would plan it this way.

I just sat up here, minding My own business . . .

Okay, so I gave the primate-thing a little push. I saw it going nowhere and I really wanted someone to talk to, at that stage of the game.

It was one of the few times I stuck My fingers in the pie.

Look what happened!

Here we go. So, you wish you'd never been born.

Cry you a river. Nobody loves you, everybody hates you, guess you'll eat some worms.

What about ME? Do you think *THIS* is a picnic for Me?

What do you think goes through *MY* mind, as I'm packing My things?

I'm thinking about Mary Shelley's *Frankenstein*, is what I'm thinking about.

I have been hanging around here for EONS, fostering a losing proposition . . . trying VERY HARD not to meddle and manipulate, giving you chance after chance . . .

On the other hand, I DO acknowledge your achievements! I'm OLD but I'm not blind! There's goodness among you and a genuine sense of charity.

Don't you think having to forsake all that is KILLING ME??

Unfortunately, we all know the history of that one bad apple. It's happening right before My very eyes! How can you do such things in front of Me, like I wasn't even there?

It boils down to this: I am not supposed to react to your behavior, because of *who I am*. My job has always been to forgive you, no matter what.

> *I am the voice of reason.*
> *I am the peace-keeper.*

Most of all, I am the Man who should look away the day you send a missile across the sky, headed for a village that lies asleep . . .

It hurts more than you could ever know, and it is not fair for you to expect Me to cover My eyes.

That's right, change the subject. Talk about children, My weakness.

Of course I love them. Without a doubt, they are My favorite.

Ah. Those tiny little fingers tying a shoelace into a twisted knot, with the tongue that darts in and out, until the feat is actually accomplished.

The young boy fishing with his grandfather for the first time. Reluctantly, he threads the worm through the hook, asking the old man if it hurts the worm.

"No," the grandfather says, but they both know that's not quite the truth.

Sacrifices are made, and that's how it is.

The fact is, children will still love Me no matter what.   If anyone will understand My hasty departure, they will.

Oh Sweet Henry, I sound like a parent, all packed and ready to leave, rationalizing the upcoming divorce . . .

"My decision to leave has nothing to do with you.

I'll see you every other weekend.

This is not your fault . . ."

I can take the children with Me, you know. I would never do it, but if I wanted to, I could . . . Lest you forget there is NOTHING I cannot do. Nothing.

I can fly to the moon on Gossamer wings.
I can hitch a ride on the tail of a comet.
I can float among the clouds on the breath of Angels.

Surely, I can take the children with Me. It would serve you right.

I'm wondering if you will be man enough (no gender bias intended) to admit to your part in all of this.

What am I thinking? You will definitely blame Me.

So what else is new?

Now, if you don't mind, I'd like to retract My offer for an audience, end this discussion, and finish the rest of My packing alone. I've got some sorting out to do and I prefer to do it in silence.

Let's see, what goes in the Goodwill pile?

The harp and the robe? I certainly don't need THEM where I'm going. They were YOUR idea, anyway. Nothing but props. Oh, what have we here . . . a staff. Definitely a non-essential.

The halo is a keeper. I could never get rid of that.

Now, please be on your way.

I mean it. I need My privacy.

I HEARD THAT! Somebody mentioned "the old timers" . . .

I'm all they've got!

Very, VERY low blow.

I can take them with Me also, so don't think you are threatening Me with an ace in the hole!

I've got My hands over My ears. I cannot hear you, so you might as well go away. You simply WILL NOT make Me change My mind. La-la-la-la LA!! I'm singing and I can't understand a word you're saying . . .

Okay, I'm closing the door! Here it goes, it's closing shut . . .

I will not be touched by sentiment. It is too late. A Divine and Generous Pedagogue simply cannot and will not be influenced by the empty words of selfish Jugheads.

Get your foot out of the door before I snap it off at the ankle.

These boots are made for walking. Out of sight, out of mind.

This hurts Me more than it does you.

I've got one last stop to make . . . don't ask Me where. It's none of your beeswax. Then I'll be off, never to return.

See you in the funny papers.

At this same point in time, on the other side of town, another old-timer is spinning a yarn . . .

It's a good one, so gather around.

The Mystery of the Dead Sea Squirrels

My name is Roger T. Hemingway, no relation.

What I am is a connoisseur a conversation,
specializin' in particular discussions where I
ain't exactly one a the participants . . . if ya
git my drift.

Eavesdroppin', is what ya'd call it.

Now, before ya go n establish a negative opinion
'bout me n my hobby, I'd like ta set the record
straight by sayin' that I mostly keep what I
hear ta myself. Ya won't find me sittin' 'round
a checkerboard blabberin' other people's
business to a buncha ol' coots, haffa which is
so deef they couldn't hear a hand grenade go
off, if it blowed up under their chair.

See, I jest take the incomin' information n file
it away fer safe keepin'. It's how I amuse
myself in my old age. Humor me . . . it's all I
got.

Anyways, I hear this n that, n the other thing:
So-n-so's got a hernia from liftin' the back end
of a Jeep Wagoneer offa his dog's tail . . .
What's-her-name's gone up North ta have the fat
sucked outta her jowls by some hotshot New York
City doctor. If that don't make a person wanna
holler jest thinkin' 'bout it . . .

. . . mainly small-town gossip that'd bore
most folks ta tears quicker'n a three credit
course in financial accountin'.

Hmmmm. Now, how do I continue on from here
without destroyin' my credibility n ruinin' my
good name, 'specially after I done everythin'
but give myself a Nobel Peace Prize?

What I do is ta come out with it, n if y'all
don't wanna listen . . . well, be off with ya.
I don't see none a ya chained to a tree.

Let's jest say my "no-tell rule" become null n
void the day I met two feisty young
whippersnappers from . . . I ain't exactly sure
where they're from. Never did say n it don't
matter anyways.

Furthermore, the participants involved ain't gonna care much, since they don't got a brain stem between em, I swear. Oh, and I'm gonna say this one thing 'bout myself before we git knee-deep in the plot. I ain't a educated man, not by any stretch a the imagination. Never even finished high school. But I ain't STUPID. So maybe I talk kinda funny and alla that, but I KNOW I talk funny. See, there's yer difference. These young men . . . *they don't know the difference. They are as dumb as a sack fulla shoe horns.*

Okay, here's the thing.

Ya got yer two brothers . . . Rudy n Titus Horne. I reckon Rudy was somewheres 'round thirteen years old, judgin' by the way the peach fuzz run rampant over his upper lip. Titus, he mighta been ten. He talked in that annoyin' soon-to-be-a-man squeak, n ya jest a soon he kep his mouth shut, til his share a the family hormones kicked in. A scrawny lookin' thing, he was. All feet n hardly no length b'tween his waist n ankles.

I become acquainted with these two future rocket
scientists in a little so-called *Antique Store*
this side a Memphis, Tennessee. Wasn't many
antiques in there though, jest a buncha ol'
junk. The boys, they was tellin' the most
outrageous tale ta my friend Leo Bachman, the
owner a said 'stablishment.

Leo, now there's another one. He's got what ya
call "alternatin' strabismus," meanin' he can
only see outta one eye at a time. Never know if
Leo is lookin' at ya, due ta how his eyes veer
off every which-a-way. I guess that's good, if
yer tryin' ta rip somebody off, or needin' ta
shoot a gun from each hand. Leo, he done both a
them things, I can promise ya that.

Anyways, Rudy . . . he's swingin' this sack a
somethin'-er-another all 'round as he's talkin',
all excited n wild-eyed.

A course, bein' who I am n doin' what I do, I
leaned an inquisitive ear in the direction a
this conversation, pretendin' ta be scrutinizin'
an ol' RCA television console fer a future
purchase.

Leo, he knew what I was doin'. The boy-wonders don't know squat from squat. They keep yammerin' away while I suck it all in like the power hose on a Hoover.

It seems the boys spent some time in the Mideast with their parents. Lived there, went ta school, blabbety-blab-blab. Dad was some kind a U.S. Embassy bigwig, obviously not too concerned about the projection of yer guided missile system that ya got over yonder in them A-rab countries. Ya know what I'm talkin' 'bout, if ya ever watch the evenin' news with Dan, whats-his-name, Rather. They got all kinds a Tommy Hawk thingamajiggers pointed at each other. Personally, I don't know how any of em git a decent night's sleep.

Okay, I'm goin' off on a tangent, which I do on occasion, mainly 'cause I don't git ta tell that many stories anymore, since I'm old n most of my friends are dead.

One day, the two brothers was hangin' out in one of them open-air-market places they got over there. Myself, you couldn't git me to eat somethin' that sat in a sun that's hotter than

the sweat offa The Devil's hind leg . . . no
sirree. Anyways, Rudy n Titus tell a how they
was pawin' through this n that, bitin' big
holes in the exotic fruit n vegetables, givin'
the shopkeepers a near heart attack.

Well, enough horseplay n they decided ta head
off fer a dip in the hotel pool. On the way,
they noticed two American men whisperin' to each
other over a display a fresh fish . . . fresh,
meanin' they wasn't flyblown an crawlin' with
maggots. Anyhow, these men was old n decrepit.
Prolly hittin' forty accordin' to Rudy . . . but
they was very well dressed, n seemingly outta
place.

Titus thinks they're spies, gittin' ready ta
retrieve a secret micro-tape from the belly of a
sea bass.

Rudy says "no." They're insurance salesmen,
scoutin' up business wherever they can.

Cautiously, the boys stroll closer.

Rudy, he's pretendin' ta be in the market fer a
nice, ripe avocado, as he leans towards the

private conversation. A course, ya could believe that 'bout Rudy, checkin' out the avocados, I mean. He's a bit on the porky side, them little do-what-sis love handles kinda oozin' over the top a his jeans. Plus, n I don't mean ta be cruel, his fingers looked like Jimmy Dean Sausages, over-stuffed n dimpled from eatin' one too many chocolate he-haws, or whatever them processed lard-cakes are called.

Titus, he squats down close ta the ground n commences ta tie his shoe, in hopes a pickin' up whatever part a the personal discussion his brother mighta missed.

By the way. I'd like ta take this opportunity, even though it has nuthin' ta do with the story line, ta wonder what kinda mother could look down at a new born baby n name it Titus?

Ya name a Great Dane Titus, or a Harley Davidson that's got a big ol' hole rusted through its exhaust pipe. Ya jest don't name a real human bein' Titus unless yer lookin' ta have every street gang in the Universe use yer own flesh n blood as a kickstand fer the resta Eternity. I know what I'm talkin' about. See, I gotta cousin who suffered with the name "Yul" his whole long life, after what's-his-name . . . ya know who I mean, the movie star with the bald head. I think he's dead . . . Holy Anchovy, I jest can't thinka the man's last name. Anyhow, can't say I know WHAT in the hollyhock my Aunt Loretta had on her mind the day her youngest plopped out on that gurney. Ya got yer Clark Gable or yer Tyrone Power, or how 'bout yer Sir Laurence Olivi-yea, if yer gonna go ga-ga over some movie star.

Yul Rueben Hemingway. Ya better be thinkin' 'bout gittin' that kid karate lessons n pronto, 'cause there's one youngun who's gonna be kung-fu-in' hisself down every dark alley.

Kids can be cruel, ya know. I'm thinkin' Titus Horne knows that fer a fact. Now what was I sayin'?

Oh yeah. Ya got the two younguns strainin' ta hear somethin' that surely weren't none a their business.

One a the ol' fossils is tellin' the other spawn-of-a-dinosaur that there was REAL MONEY ta be found out yonder in the Caves of a . . .

Gobbledegook. The Caves of Gobbledegook.

Hidden deep in the bowels a these caves were the mysterious n elusive Dead Sea . . .

Dead Sea . . . what??

"Sounds like *Squirrels*," Titus whispers ta his brother.

DEAD SEA SQUIRRELS!! Rudy, he moves his heavy load jest a tad closer, so's he can catch every word the strangers are sayin'.

Well. These Dead Sea Squirrels could reap a small fortune. It seems The World has been searchin' fer this particular treasure fer hundreds a years! As a matter a fact, missin' n controversial segments of ancient history were certain ta be revealed, once the squirrels were found n exposed! Fame n fortune awaits those who retrieve em. We're talkin' picture on the

cover a *Entertainment Weekly*, plus a spot on
David Letterman, not to mention the . . .

Brynner. That was the baldheaded guy's name,
Brynner. I knew it'd come ta me.

Not ta mention the opportunity ta spend a week
in Electronic World, buyin' every CD ROM
whatchamajigger, with yer nekid ladies that can
do a back bend right there on the screen a yer
computer. See, there's money, lots of it, in
the recovery a The Dead Sea Squirrels.

The two men had DEFINITE plans ta be the said
"retrievers" a the aforementioned objects.
There was no doubt 'bout that. As they
whispered back n forth in the open-air market,
Rudy n Titus hovered near by, latchin' onta bits
n pieces a their secret discussion . . . knowin'
this was a job fer two young boys, not a couple
a antiques that prolly couldn't even walk fast,
or bend over ta tie their shoes.

One a the old men takes outta map, n unfolds it
ta show his friend.

Rudy can't see it. He's wider than he is tall.

Titus, no way can he even catch a glimpse.

It don't matter. The boys are sure they know where the Gobbledegook Caves are. There jest weren't that many caves in the area they could be talkin' about!

This was an adventure that would surely give em the money they needed fer the afore alluded to Virtual-Reality-Strip-Tease!

So, as to git a healthy head start on the IBM Executive clones, Rudy n Titus hightailed it outta there, racin' as fast as their short little legs could take em, to pack what all they'd need ta make this a comfortable n profitable expedition.

Now, I don't mean ta veer off in another direction again, but I jest have ta comment on the seemingly "don't-give-a-mind" attitude of the mother a these two boys.

Here ya gotta couple a youngsters, hardly outta diapers, rushin' home all in a huff. They're packin' equipment n food in a feverish frenzy.

Titus, he claims his mama don't say word one, like "Where are ya goin' n when are ya comin' back?" She don't do nuthin' but pitch in n help em pack! Don't it RING A BELL that there's some major travelin' goin' on here, with yer TOOLS n FLASHLIGHTS n SLEEPIN' BAGS? What does she think, that they're preparin' fer a Mideastern, A-Rab, Boy Scout Jamboree kinda thing?

Ya either gotta mama who really needed a vacation from these two seeds a Satan, or a woman who don't give a lot a credence ta the 1-800-IM-ABUSED Hotline. Not that they got such a thing over there. From what I hear, the A-Rab father rules the roost n can do jest 'bout anythin' he wants ta his family. Shoot em all dead in their tracks, if he wants. Say ya got yerself a wife who don't take ta cookin' . . . BLAM-O! Blow her head off! Ya gotta couple a kids who make the mistake a gittin' kinda mouthy, load up again n send em where they'll meet Elvis. That's jest the way yer A-rabs do things. I'm not sayin' it's right, I'm simply sayin' it's their way.

A course, the Horne family wasn't Arabian n they were only there on business so I guess the

murder-yer-family-in-cold-blood rules didn't
apply ta them. And I'm also pretty sure there
ain't a hotline fer abused children, but there
sure as heck should be, jest fer such an
occasion as this.

Now, I know yer thinkin' I've gone way offa the
deep end with this, but I call shippin' the
fruit a yer womb off ta Lord only knows where
with a "don't let the door slam against yer
hind-end on the way out" attitude, plain n
simple neglect. I guess maybe I'm jest bein' a
little sensitive, seein' how me n the late Mrs.
Hemingway was never blessed with children. We
tried plenty hard, that's a fact. No, what we
finally done is fill the void with a cocker
spaniel named Stumpy n two blue-eyed cats
someone pitched from their car window on the way
outta town. Worth good money, them cats, n The
Missus loved em ta death. She named em Laurel n
Hardy, even though they was both lady cats,
'cause one was dumber than a soup ladle n the
other spent her time bein' frustrated. See,
Hardy would find the mouse n kill it, then
Laurel would eat it. Myself, I don't figure
that's bein' TOO STUPID . . . I think THAT'S
being pretty darn smart, but ya couldn't tell

The Missus that. She said Laurel would never
know what mouse meat tasted like if it wasn't
fer Hardy.

It weren't worth the air time, spoutin' off my
opinion. Not once Mrs. Hemingway made her mind
up 'bout somethin'.

Pets hardly replace a child. I know that. I
ain't a total moron, but they give us a lotta
joy jest the same.

Tis neither here nor there, I reckon n once
again, I wandered offa the trail. Fact is,
Rudy n Titus prepared fer a lengthy trip inta
the desert n their mama done mosta the packin',
jeez Louise.

Okay, off they go. It's hot n steamy n even
though the boys had explored the area before,
when they shoulda been in school, the landscape
was still very foreign n not what they was used
to. See, caves in the Middle East ain't like
the caves a, let's say, South Dakota. No way.
Can't compare em . . . it's like apples n
oranges.

They had ta trudge through miles a desert, fight wind n sand, not ta mention avoidin' unfamiliar varmints a the deadly kind . . . snakes n scorpions n what-have-ya. Plus ya got yer heat index which pushes over the hundred degree mark come high noon.

Now, the way Rudy n Titus tells it, they ventured off inta the desert, headin' straight fer the caves on pure intuition. It was a treacherous journey n Titus recalls that at one point, he wanted ta forsake all the fame n fortune that would come from The Squirrels. Rudy, hisself, had second thoughts on more than one occasion, 'specially after ponderin' the food situation from a "what if there's an emergency" point a view. Like "what if" they got lost or caught in a sand storm? "What if" it took longer'n they thought ta find the squirrels? "What if" the two old men took an extra dose a their Bayer Arthritis Pain Formula n by some miracle, got ta the caves first, n snatched up them squirrels? Holy Horn-dog, Rudy n Titus could spend days wanderin' 'round in a futile frenzy. In any event, there was a definite concern over the limited supply a Little Debbie Chocolate Covered Wax-Wads, yes indeed there was. The panic was short-lived, however, as the visions of a hand-held Virtual Reality Game Boy crep slowly back inta Rudy's immediate thoughts . . . all them virtual-villians blowin' the heads offa this one n that one, blood squirtin' out every which-a-way. Not ta mention the nekid lady with a tattoo of a tulip on her thigh, all ya gotta do is git her shorts off. It was simply too grand an opportunity ta pass up. Onward n upward.

Hold the phone jest a minute folks . . . There's a commotion goin' on somewheres outside, someone yellin' n screamin' . . . Sounds like a ravin' maniac 'bout ta bust a vessel. Think I heard him calling someone a "Jughead," if THAT ain't rude. Let me go close the front door. I can hardly hear myself think. Lord knows I can't keep my mind focused fer more'n a second or two, as it is.

I'm back . . . where was I? Oh, yes.

I don't know how they done it, I swear I don't, but they come upon The Caves in Question after the end a the first day. Seems mind-bogglin' ta me. Anyways, they battled the blowin' sand with the stamina a two old desert camels n actually claimed ta have entered the first cave in time ta fix themselves some dinner.

Titus swore he wasn't scared in the slightest. Their flashlights provided enough light ta take the edge offa the eerie darkness, n he bragged 'bout wantin' ta go deeper, where "the real action" hadda be.

Rudy, much older n wiser, wanted ta take his time n explore the area slowly n in detail. After all, neither boy had ever seen a Dead Sea Squirrel before, n it would prove ta be tragic indeed if the treasure was overlooked in haste.

Rudy won his case. It was decided the first course a action was ta make a fire. (Caves are notoriously cold, not ta mention crawlin' with yer cave-creatures, n such. Everyone knows a roarin' fire will keep away even yer most ferocious varmint.)

Ha! Do you think these future Harvard Law School candidates ever thought 'bout fire-buildin' material back when they was packin' the butterscotch ying-yangs n barbecue pork rinds? Not that they coulda hauled a cord a wood across the desert, strapped on their backs . . . I've got enough working upstairs ta realize that. Myself, I woulda grabbed me a couple a them artificial-petroleum-product, Dura Flame log things . . . n don't tell me they ain't got such a item over there in Oil Country, 'cause I know better. What they are is a roll a yer compressed oil-residue. Same stuff they put in nerve gas. Jest read the package.

Well anyways, accordin' ta the story, the cave was a bit light in the timber department. Jest yer bat droppin's n maybe a couple of sticks, which God only knows if they *REALLY WAS* sticks, coulda been bones, is what I say.

So, there they are, plannin' a big ol' fire with nuthin' but nuthin'. Rudy scoured every crack n crevice a that first cave with the flashlight, upwards, downwards, cross-wise.

Titus began kickin' the livin' bejesus outta the floor a the cave, takin' huge gouges outta the dirt . . . What in the doo-dad was the little brain surgeon thinkin'? Like maybe there would be fire logs buried somewheres under the surface? Kicked n kicked, so he's tellin' my friend Leo, when all of a sudden he smacks inta somethin' that 'bout snapped his toes right offa their hinges.

He calls fer his brother n together they begin diggin' with a spade they had packed fer jest such an occasion. One holds the flashlight, the other one digs. Could be The Dead Sea Squirrels, don't ya know.

Rudy gets all depressed n somber-like when he's tellin' this part. What they find is a long cylinder tube, maybe brass or somethin' like that. From how they describe it, it's ornate with all kindsa carvin's etched inta the metal, from top ta bottom. Titus pulls a plug from the top a the tube, n retrieves what he calls "nuthin' but a buncha old, wrinkled papers, covered with squiggly lines." Smelled bad, too, he said. Like a ol' bait bucket.

Are y'all hearin' me? ***"Old papers covered with squiggly lines." Mother a Pearl, that's all I gotta say. Mother a Pearl.***

They kicked n dug some more. Lo n behold,
there's more a these tubes. Some made outta
animal hide, some made outta a substance neither
boy could 'dentify. Prolly ivory or somethin'
on that order, be still my heart. All the
containers are packed fulla rolled up papers.

Now, maybe there's no squirrels ta be found in
this particular spot, which surely was a major
disappointment, but what ya got here is some
excellent fire-buildin' material. Wad it all
up, toss in the sticks (or bones, ha, ha, ha) n
there ya go! Nice n toasty, plus a way ta cook
them hamburgers ya brought along, all oozin'
with salmonella n botulism from being hauled
across a desert that's hotter than the hubs a
Hell.

I'm laughin' my head off, ya see, as they
continue on with this pitiful saga. It ain't
really funny . . . I know that. It's pathetic.
I guess it's one a them instances where you
hadda be there, watchin' n listenin' ta the
story unfold like a old Columbo movie. See,
Columbo has a way a makin' a person laugh
through a entire murder investigation, even
though there is nuthin' remotely humorous 'bout

murder. That's what ya got goin' on here. Only
Rudy n Titus ain't got even a tenth the brain
that Columbo's got. They ain't tryin' ta be
funny or clever. They're as serious as a
anurizm.

So, the Horne brothers built 'emselves a ragin'
inferno from the "useless rolls a paper," happy
ta be warm, even more happy ta have a way ta
cook their food. 'Specially the chunky one.
He'd be, whatayacallit, goin' inta sugar shock
without sustenance on a hourly basis. Matter a
fact, he ate a Milky Way bar while tellin' this
story. Had ta do it, couldn't live without it.
Never once asked his brother does he want a
bite, neither.

Okay, so the boys go on ta explain how they
looked 'round the area one more time, before
callin' it a day. They unrolled their sleepin'
bags, n settled close ta the fire. Accordin' ta
Rudy, they was asleep in minutes. (I don't buy
that one, 'specially with yer bats n nocturnal
creepy-crawlies hoverin' about. I'll bet they
was up all night.)

Now, the next mornin' they packed up n headed deeper inta the cave. Rudy claims it got wider n funnier smellin', plus the ceilin' rose "way up, almost a mile." A course that's jest the exaggerated perception of a boy with no concept a distance. I'd guess the ceilin' weren't no more'n fifty feet high, tops.

They told Leo 'bout how they seen strange carvin's etched inta the walls as the beams a their flashlights skimmed the area. Titus thought they was lookin' at artwork done by Aliens from Outer Space. Yer baldheaded, boney-fingered, Sigorney-Weaver-type alien whose innards could burst open at any moment with droolin', slobberin', three-headed serpents. That's how Titus described it, anyway.

Unfortunately, we all know how the movie industry has gone n shattered the respectable image a today's average alien. I can 'test ta that 'cause I once had the pleasure a comin' face ta face with a REAL, LIVE exter-testeral. It was back in '58. Me n The Missus was fishin' on Linkhorn Lake, when outta the sky comes this big ol' saucer, jest a hummin' n a buzzin' over our heads. Mrs. Hemingway was so scared she 'bout popped herself a goiter, but after a few minutes she calmed down n enjoyed the moment.

The saucer veered over ta the left a us n landed in a clearin'. Sounds like a ol' flyin' saucer cliché, I know. But that's 'xactly what it done, landed in a clearin'.

Well, out comes three watchamacallit space creatures . . . heads the size of a hassock. They were buck nekid but none a their parts was THAT obvious. Believe me, The Missus was lookin'. I recall thinkin' they looked mighty sickly, greenish in color n very thin.   Anyhow, one comes over to us n says he wants a hunk a our hair. No problem there . . . I grabs a fistful n so don't Mrs. Hemingway, we hand it over n off they go. I'm thinkin' they musta been speakin' through one a them language-translator, voice-simulator-implants like ya see on Star Trek. See, how else could they a communicated with us?

I done it again. If I ain't nuthin' but a big ol' bag a wind. I know you'll forgive me 'cause we've got this far. Furthermore, everyone loves a "alien story." How could ya not??

Let's see, where was I? Oh, yes.

Rudy found a old "coffee cup" n several "really
neat cereal dishes" buried in one corner.
Titus, he thinks it would be great fun ta kinda
skeet shoot with these particular items, n talks
Rudy into pitchin' em into the air, while he
tries to bring em down with rocks. What the
heck, if ya git my drift. Yer prolly only
talkin' 'bout dishes that maybe Cleopatra or
Juliass Cezar ate offa. Ha! Then they dug some
more, n whaddya think . . . MORE USELESS
CYLINDERS A STINKY OL' PAPER . . . PRAISE THE
GOOD LORD, 'CAUSE THEY'D NEED ANOTHER CAMPFIRE
COME SUPPER TIME!

The boys admitted ta being thankful fer the fire
kindlin', yet they was gittin' anxious ta locate
the precious Dead Sea Squirrel, knowin' the two
geriatric businessmen would soon be on the
scene. And what if these squirrels was SO
VALUABLE that they was worth committin' MURDER
over? The old men could sneak up on em in the
middle a the night n shoot the boys dead! Who'd
ever know? See, I blame their mama, once again,
fer not takin' a interest in what her sons was

doin' n where they was goin'. In this day n age, anything can happen. Jest watch yer *Hard Copy* n skim through yer *National Enquirer*, fer beans sakes. Anyways, foul play was definitely a possibility n Rudy says they started diggin' with a vengeance.

What in the blue blazes . . . more old dishes, some heavy metal pieces a whatever, shaped inta this n that, n a course, OLD PAPER.

Titus, the little pinhead, crushed everythin' that would break. It was fun n soon he forgot 'bout the squirrels n got lost in the act a destruction, turnin' each n every artifact inta ancient dust.

Now, I have ta tell ya that I am no longer pretendin' ta be interested in the ol' RCA console. No ma'am. I'm as close ta these two Einsteins as a flea on a pit bull's hind end. Ta tell ya the truth, I was quiverin' inside. See, I'm half expectin' ta hear how they found two clay tablets buried in the bowels a them caves, which they clapped together like cymbals. Or maybe how they dug up a silver chalice that looked like nuthin' so they banged it inta a

twisted   pretzel with a rock, jest fer somethin'
to do.

Ol' Leo, he's jest lookin' down at his watch,
kinda eye-ballin' the door, maybe hopin' someone
will come in n disrupt this conversation, which
ta him, is goin' nowheres. I can tell he
couldn't care less 'bout what's in the sack.
He's got no clue as ta what's happenin' here
since he's pretty much a fiesta-ware kind-a-guy.
Cracked Looney Tunes jelly glasses n World's
Fair ashtrays. Whatever these younguns are
sellin' is a little or no interest ta him. He'd
jest as soon talk "made in Japan" teacups with
Viola Preston. But Viola Preston never come in
ta save him that day, so he jest stood there
behind the cash register, prayin' fer a rescue.

Ya gotta hang on ta yer hat a minute while I
check out all the howlin'. Enough is enough.
Holy Succotash, the walls are a-shakin'.

Don't see a soul. Must be someone on another
street, yellin' through one a them megaphone
doosey-wap-sees. I'm surprised no one's called
911. This here is yer major disturbin' a the
peace. Nuthin' I can do 'bout it now . . . not

while I'm midst story tellin'. If I git off beat, I'm good fer nuthin'.

Anyways, you got Rudy yakkin' away 'bout how his brother is disposin' a everythin' in sight, admittin' that he hisself smashed a "flower pot n a mixin' bowl," but that's all." Kinda braggin' 'bout it. At some point, Rudy claims they emptied this particular cave of all its contents n moved on through a narrow passage ta another area.

Accordin' ta Titus, this cave "stunk like a bologna sandwich that's been sittin' on the radiator fer a week or so." It was the coldest n darkest of anywheres they'd been, n Rudy says it was lucky they had a stockpile a "useless ol' papers" . . . a course, ta use fer a ragin' campfire. Lucky fer them, there was even more leather tubes jam-packed with "fire kindlin," layin' all 'round, not even buried! Before they commenced their search fer the squirrel, Rudy built hisself a rip-roarin' blazin' holocaust that singed off his eyebrows. We're talkin' barn-burner, fer corn's sake!

Some eatin' went on, at this point, n then
sleep. See, they don't have a clue as ta what
time it is 'cause neither genius-boy wore a
watch. They don't even know if it's day or
night. What they're doin' is playin' it by ear.
Sleepin' when they're tired n eatin' when
they're hungry. Plus they're keeping their
eyes n ears open at all times, fer the two
"squirrel-hunters" they seen back in the
marketplace. Time was of the essence . . . this
priceless treasure would be theirs, at all cost.

Titus woke up before Rudy, n began rootin'
'round with a flashlight. The fire had dwindled
down to a smolderin' pile a ashes, n he recalls
bein' cold. They're deep inta the caverns by
now. Even in the desert a cave'll git chilly
enough to freeze yer nose holes shut. I know
that from listenin' ta my Uncle Roy talk 'bout
how he hid in some cave in the Sahara during one
a yer World Wars, don't remember which.
Colder'n a hound's tooth, that's what my Uncle
Roy said.

Now, Titus finds enough ol' papers ta git the
fire goin' again . . . Holy Humpback, ya gotta
know each n every one a those priceless relics

hadda burst inta flame like The Waco Compound,
if THAT wasn't a pitiful shame.

Okay, so he's roamin' about n Rudy's still
catchin' some shut-eye. Titus, he says the
smell was REALLY BAD n he jest couldn't figure
out where it was comin' from.

All of a sudden, he looks up in the air. It's
up there . . . the stench, that is. How the
little dim-wit-twitty knows that fer sure, I
can't say. Fact is, it's waftin' down from the
ceilin' a the cave, comin' from the rotting
carcass a . . .

Yessirree, yer one step ahead a me. That smell
come from the elusive Dead Sea Squirrel, all
festerin' n oozin' with slime. At least that's
how Titus tells it. I hadda believe what he was
sayin' 'cause if this long-winded tale was goin'
where I thought it was, said squirrel was in the
sack Rudy was so nonchalantly flingin' about.
I'm quick ta assume that 'cause I don't mind
sayin' I could detect a whiff a somethin' rank n
foul seepin' inta the air . . . Smelled it fer
jest about the entire length a the story but
didn't say nuthin'. See, ya never know what

physical ailment somebody might have that would give off an offensive stench. Ya wouldn't wanna embarrass a person by sniffin' 'round where they're standin', or makin' a remark 'bout said odor jest in passin'. That's plain insensitive. I know 'bout these things first hand. My sister's youngest, ya'd better be sure yer sittin' downwind from that young lady. Reeks like horse liniment. Can't help it, though, n we all know enough ta keep our thoughts ta ourselves. Somethin' ta do with her pancreas.

Okay, I'm ramblin' again. So what else is new? The point is, Titus looked up fer jest a second n right there at that moment knows he's hit the mother lode. It's The Squirrel, all right, n what he does is go over ta Rudy, wake him up, n both boys commence formulatin' a plan a action. The Squirrel is pretty high up, dead a course, so it ain't goin' nowheres, but still ya gotta figure out how ta git it down.

Apparentley, the animal was hangin' from a bungycord-kinda-contraption. Ya know, like yer Mexican piñata. He says it seemed ta be wrapped in a cocoon-like shell: little feet n tail

pokin' through. That's how come they knew it
was a squirrel.

Now, I know what yer thinkin'. Yer thinkin'
this is all a royal crock a the highest-grade
hooey there ever was. There ain't no such thing
as a Dead Sea Squirrel!

See, that's where yer wrong. There's a
squirrel, all right. Course, moron-boys think
they got one thing when they really got another,
if ya git my drift.

Well, let me finish the story as I heard it, n
you'll see what I mean . . . if ya haven't
caught on already, that is.

They can't figure out how ta git The Squirrel
down. Titus, he stands on Rudy's shoulders.
Not near high enough. Rudy, he stands on
Titus's shoulders. Rudy thought they was a lot
taller that way, whaddaya expect from a
idiot-child like him. They don't have a single
piece a campin' equipment that'll reach that
far. Prolly needed a dagblasted tent pole, or
maybe even two or three tied tagether ta whack
that thing offa the bungy. Never mind that Rudy

n Titus Horne go campin' without a tent. Never
mind that at all.

Titus, he's the guy with "the arm" . . . the guy
who's been pitchin' n hurlin' everythin' in
sight. So's what he does is he starts heavin'
this n that up at the animal. Tools, cans a
food, flashlights. It's the only hope they got
a gitttin' it down, ya see.

Rudy claims his brother whipped a screw driver
straight through the bungy, and the whole
kit-n-kaboodle dropped ta the floor, plop.

The boys gather 'round, the beams a their
flashlights aimed straight on The Squirrel,
neither one brave enough ta pick the thing up
fer a closer look.

Rudy kicks it with his foot. Titus flips it
over with the screw driver. It's obvious
they've gotta break open the cocoon-like-thing
which, a course, is slicked over with a glaze a
somethin' really putrid.

Now, ya got me here, 'cause the way the boys
tell it, they're 'fraid ta touch the thing.

Rudy, I know fer a fact, he'd clean n fillet a bucket full a sea slugs, if that's all there was ta eat. Titus, he's spent every moment he's been in the caves diggin' n probin' 'round in dirt that's gotta be infested with some a yer grosser life forms. Holy Hammerhock, they both been sleepin' on top a bat dung n whatever else walked or slithered by n squatted. It's hard ta believe a little slime would make em squeamish.

Anyways, they played 'round with the thing til Rudy finally gathered enough courage ta slit the shell with his knife. Inside, sure enough, is the rest a The Squirrel, still intact n ready ta be sold ta the highest bidder.

Leo, he ain't said hardly one word since the boys started the story. Now, however, he speaks up. He wants ta know what a Dead Sea Squirrel looks like . . . not that he's really THAT interested. See, I know he's not gonna buy the thing. It's jest not up his alley, n like I said before, he don't know diddly 'bout what's REALLY goin' on.

I do. I know 'xactly what's happenin'. Maybe I'm nuthin' more than a backwoods hick, who keeps his money pinned ta his undershirt (Now don't git any ideas 'bout robbin' me. I can pull outta gun, aim, n split the long hairs in yer nose down the middle before ya can kiss a fool), but I read n listen, n believe me when I tell ya, I know what's goin' on here.

So. Rudy starts ta describe the animal, not realizin' all he's gotta do is OPEN THE SACK. As ya know, we ain't talkin' "MENSA" membership.

He goes on ta say how there's fur n scales on the thing. Little slits under its ears. Gills, is what they are. Webbed feet, but still kinda "paw-like." A bushy tail, a course, n a pouch on its belly like a kangaroo. Titus talked 'bout "little wings" that poked outta its shoulder blades . . . feathered n scrawny. A beak-like mouth, with teeth . . .

Obviously, nuthin' like a squirrel.

Yet everythin' like a squirrel.

Well, let's git ta the nitty gritty. Ya can call "it" whatever ya want; fact is we're dealin' with somethin' that scientists been lookin' fer since the day they all decided we didn't evolve from a brussel sprout. Now, we're not even talkin' missin' link, 'cause that refers to a primate-connection. No, this here's different. What ya got here is yer definitive proof that all forms a life come from a common bein'. And I ain't talkin' 'bout one a them Brazilian Shrew thingamabobs, like what ya hear 'bout on The Discovery Channel. The Squirrel's definitely more complex n THAT.

See, all a this is nuthin' new ta me. I believed in such a theory mosta my life, ever since the day I caught a glimpse a Sylvia Hawkshaw standin' nekid in front a the Rexall Drug, singin' *Swannee, How I Love Ya, How I Love Ya* at the top a her lungs . . . broke loose from the "whacko farm," is what she done. Anyways, if ya hadda gotta good look at this woman's anatomy the way I did, ya surely would agree with me 'bout how we all come from a single ancestor. Yes indeed ya would.

The rest a the story is even more excitin', if ya can believe that's even possible. The boys take the dead animal back ta wherever it is they're livin' . . . Wish I could think of

exactly where they said it was, I wanna say
"Bhuna-Bynadhi," or somethin' like that. It was
one a yer Middle Eastern townships, that's all I
can tell ya.

Their mama tells em ta get the stinky thing
outta the house before she grinds it up in the
garbage disposal. See, I didn't think yer A-rab
countries had garbage disposals n such. I been
wrong before, I'll admit ta that.

So now Mama Horne wants the animal outta her
sight. (This woman is no doubt what the writers
fer Hallmark have in mind when they're whippin'
up poetry fer their "mother's day collection",
ha, ha, ha.) Rudy and Titus gotta hide The
Squirrel someplace safe. Someplace where it'll
keep, meanin' outta the heat.

Bingo! They wrap it up in white paper, n stuff
it way in back a the freezer. Arabians got
freezers, jest like us Americans. Can hardly
believe it when ya take a look at yer CNN and
all ya see is mud huts clutterin' the
countryside. (Now that I think 'bout it, maybe
that's India).

Okay, accordin' ta Rudy, several months go by n Mama never finds the white package in the freezer. (If it's anything like my freezer, it's simply a place ta store 'bout twenty or thirty a them blue imitation ice-things, the kind ya put in yer cooler, n such. Also, loaves a bread from the bakery outlet.) It's time ta head back ta the States . . . whatever assignment Dad was doin' fer the government was over. Titus says they put The Squirrel in a Hefty bag, stick it in a knapsack, n carry it on the plane . . . never got stopped or searched or nuthin'. What luck. Once me n The Missus (God rest her soul) "got screwed over" by one a them "you jest won a FREE trip ta Cancun, Mexico" crocks a sheep dip, n if them custom horehounds don't dump every last piece a our clothin' all over the table fer everyone to gander as they walked by . . . rootin' 'round like they was lookin' fer the Hope Diamond. Like me n Mrs. Hemingway LOOK like Hope Diamond kinda people. Git down there Mexico way n find out yer "luxurious accommodations" is a utility shed with a mattress in it. Yer "three meals a day" ain't no more'n a paper plate smolderin' with Montezuma's revenge. Never spent so much time

on a toilet in my whole life. If you wanna call
it a toilet. Now, *there's* another story.

Okay, like I was sayin', they git The Squirrel
back inta the good ol' U.S. of A. and start
lookin' fer a way ta unload it; fer big bucks, a
course. Took it here n there, showin' it ta
this one n that one. Even took it to a priest,
Titus said. See, the priest has got half a
brain n knows, like me, what's laid out before
him. I can see him now, all nervous n jerky,
plannin' an immediate disposal a said Squirrel.
You gotta know that this here animal would
surely take the wind outta the sails a yer
pompous religious sorts, shinin' the bright
light a truth on the Adam n Eve theory. Yer
Catholics don't stray a hair from THAT belief,
not a HAIR. If they do, they're doomed ta fry
in the blisterin' pits a East Hades, nowhere to
run, nowhere to hide. Now, where was I? Oh,
yes.

The priest wants The Squirrel in the worst way.
Wants ta give it a quick funeral, like I said
before. Titus says he offered em ten bucks, not
a penny more, n by the way, makes em swear on
the Pope's big hat that they won't tell anyone

else 'bout their find. Rudy, he could be missin' a chromosome er two, but there's enough goin' on top-side to alert the little man with a red flag. Ten bucks . . . no ma'am. All the priest hadda do was turn his head three degrees west, n them two younguns snatched their package n hightailed it outta there. When yer ten n thirteen years old, there's jest so much you'll do in the name a The Lord God Almighty.

Well, it seems no one else wants ta listen ta the story a how The Squirrel come ta be in their possession . . . Who'd believe em anyways, is what yer prolly thinkin'. Let's face it, I had my doubts 'bout the whole long-winded tale too, but thankfully, I stuck around ta the very end.

Which is where we are now. At the very end.

See, ol' Leo, he's sick to death a squirrel stories n has casually drifted off towards a pile a moldy *National Geographics*. Myself, I can't fer the life a me figure out why in the hip-hop a man would take up precious shelf space with a buncha old magazines. He only wants a quarter fer 'em, n what they do is SIT THERE makin' yer eyes water every time ya come inta the store. Maybe Leo Bachman's been without a woman too long n' gets hisself a cheap thrill from lookin' at all them half-naked African ladies hoppin' 'round with nuthin' on but a leopard skin diaper. Old, REALLY OLD *National Geographics* is famous fer such revealin' photographs. Personally, I'd git more of a tingle watchin' Helen Bortfeather washin' bird hockey offa the hood a her car. She's a good bender-over, Helen Bortfeather.

So what ya got left is me, Rudy n Titus n the animal.

I offer em a hundred dollars fer The Squirrel. A course by now it's laid out on the counter like a fillet o' fish, smellin' jest as bad. Never you mind, I see the potential before me . . . don't care if it smells like the Hudson River on garbage day.

The Elusive Dead Sea Squirrel

Quicker n you could whistle Dixie, Rudy n Titus
Horne grab the said cash-offer n out they go.
Nope, a hundred bucks surely ain't gonna buy ya
a Super-Nintendo Gameboy. Not in this day n
age. What it'll buy em is a two weeks supply a
marshmallow Yo-Yo's, fortified with yer high
fructose corn syrup, soy lecithin, n yer
hydrogenated cottonseed oil. (If I hadda say in
these two young fellas diet, there'd be no more
ingestion of the afore described
heart-attack-in-a-box. See, they're young but
them arteries are already commencin' ta plug up.
My nephew, Albert C. Hemingway, got hisself a
rotor-rooterin' he'll likely never fergit with
one a them coat hanger things they ram up yer
groin an inta yer neck. Only thirty-two years

ol'! Ate eggs n sausage every mornin', then
smoked hisself maybe a whole pack a
Chesterfields fer dessert, which we all know
ain't good fer ya, neither. All I'm sayin' is
ya gotta start early, watchin' yer diet. Yer
food manufacturers are gonna jam-pack whatever
cheap, artery-cloggin' grease they can git away
with. Palm oil, watch out fer THAT one.)

Heavenly Mother, I have REALLY gone astray.
Burns yer hide, don't it, 'specially when the
story's jest 'bout done.

Anyways, the point is I know I got the better
deal. I gotta piece a Creation, n I don't wanna
git on Phil Donahue or the like. Nor am I
lookin' fer a Pulitzer Prize, or an endowment ta
some Yuppie University in my honor. (Although a
gold plaque with my name on it, situated
somewheres on Princeton University's campus,
would send my goody-two-shoes brother-in-law
inta orbit, seein' how he's some hot dog
professor at afore mentioned school. Always
thought he was better n any one a the
Hemmingways, even his own sister, may she rest
in peace.)

I'm gonna put The Squirrel somewheres safe, along with my unicorn n fire-breathin', razor-backed dragon . . .

Ha, ha, only kiddin' . . .

Or not.

Well, the story don't end quite yet. I hear local scuttlebutt that yer two Horne brothers took off on another wild adventure, not too long after the previously described exchange.

It seems that while ridin' the subway, they overheard a couple a college students discussin' yer Lost Continent Of Atlantis . . . Lord only knows what part a the conversation they heard. Prolly *the lost treasure part.*

They heard all they needed ta hear, n off they went. Bought a bus ticket n headed south. Yep, yer basic beeline . . . straight ta GEORGIA!

These fellas really gotta git their mama ta scrape the wax outta their ears with one a them watchamacallit, bobbie pins.

I'll tell ya what, though. I've got half a mind ta climb on a Greyhound n track em down. Ya know, see what they come up with. I wouldn't mind forkin' over another hundred dollars. Me n the boys might 'stablish a mutual admiration society . . . Me admirin' their strange way a makin' somethin' outta nuthin', n them admirin' my generosity.

You folks have gotta excuse me, there's someone at my door. Maybe it's the "screamer." Let me gander through my peep hole.

Looks like that rock singer . . . what's-his-name. The one who jest died awhile back. Had his picture plastered all over every paper in town . . . Jerry Hoochamajigger Garcia. Yup, that's who it looks like, standing there with a suit case.

Prolly sellin' water sof'ners.

Anyways, gotta go let him in n see what's what. I need me a new water sof'ner, the one I got leaks like The Titanic.

It's been swell talkin' to ya. Maybe we'll git together again sometime n I'll tell ya 'bout the time I got Bigfoot ta help me push my Nash Rambler up the side a Mount Rushmore. Now, THAT'S a story. So long, fer now.

I'm comin', I'm comin' . . .

Hang onta yer . . .

HALO??*?*?*?*?

98

One day later . . .

<u>God Came Back on a Wednesday</u>

So I'm over it. Don't stand there with your mouth open;

. . . help Me with my things

I was *NOT* wrong. God is *NEVER* wrong. I simply over-reacted.

Even if I WERE wrong, which I wasn't, but even if I WERE, you have
no right to gloat. Gloating is not good, considering I'm still packed.

As a matter of fact, I think I'll keep My suitcase right here by the door.

I want to see improvement.

I want to see enlightenment.

I want to see remorse.

I want to gaze into those Jughead eyes of yours . . .

. . . and see surrender.

Is that asking too much?

I don't know what came over Me, out there in the cosmosphere. I was just cruising along, thinking about how peaceful life would be, enjoying the great weight that had just been lifted . . .

Suddenly, I had a vision. A man with a tanned face, hair plugs and very large teeth flashed before me. There was a closet full of Armani suits and Cole Haan wing tips, not to mention a fleet of Bentleys in assorted colors. On Sundays, he conducted services from the bow of a ninety foot yacht, directing you to send all of your extra cash to P. O. Box 336, Dallas, Texas.

You were frantically calling his ***Save-A-Soul Hotline*** for $5.99 a minute.

When he spoke to you "in tongues," which of course, was nothing more than several choruses of *Obla-dee Obla-dah,* his head kind of spun around on its axis. Very impressive.

THIS was my replacement and he moved in before My sheets even got cold. Now, please tell Me how I could allow someone with NO

CREDENTIALS, whatsoever, to sneak in the back door, in the middle of the night, and take over MY JOB . . . I think not.

Okay, okay . . . I admit I was eager to unload the position to even the talk show hucksters. I was mad. Very, very mad. It happens.

But THIS GUY was so . . .

Slick. *Slicker than the Brylcreem in James Dean's pompadour.*

Don't think I didn't wonder, for a fleeting moment, if you didn't deserve to be blind-sided by a fast-talking, long-toothed charlatan. Ha! THAT would serve you right!

I couldn't do it to the children. Or the old timers, a breath away from knocking on My door . . .

I took The Squirrel with Me, you know. Paid a visit to Mr. Roger T. Hemingway, no relation, on my way out of town. I had thoughts of introducing The Squirrel to a new environment . . . I don't know . . . out there beyond *all-there-is*. Maybe to give life another chance.

It just didn't seem right. Furthermore, I'd be ignoring My own advice: the "it's not nice to fool Mother Nature" advice, putting any future attempt to establish credibility in grave jeopardy.

I've got enough problems. So The Squirrel and I returned. Please don't make Me regret it . . . which reminds Me. I must return the

out beyond all-there-is

animal to its rightful owner. The man has quite a collection.

Let Me sum it up in another little ditty :

> I am the Old Man from Forever,
> Who has learned that you *never* say "never."

> I'm not giving My job,
> to an over-dressed clod.

> We'll just have to go through this together.

(However, getting too cocky will make all offers null and void.)

Anyway, I've decided to bite the bullet.

I'll take Prozac. I'll . . . breathe in a paper bag.

I'll give you ten million years to shape up or ship out, and *THAT'S* My final offer.

P. S. Please don't make Me wear a dress. *I like My old wardrobe.*

* * * * *

<h1 style="text-align:center"><u>Epilogue</u></h1>

Associated Press; July 17, 1996

Two young brothers, claiming to have traveled to Atlanta to find an ancient continent believed to have perished beneath the sea thousands of years ago, miraculously located said treasure while snorkeling in Lake Lanier.

Rudy and Titus Horne were underwater, looking for "fishing lures and loose change" when they spotted a volcanic-like structure poking from the floor of the lake. It is reported that when investigated further, artifacts and remains of the ancient city were indeed confirmed as authentic and were brought up by a salvaging team hired by one Roger T. Hemingway, no relation.

One source tells us that he gave the Horne Brothers one hundred dollars for the find.

While being interviewed by a local southern reporter, the boys were jokingly asked to consider making the missing "Jammy Hoffa" their next project. Rudy and Titus apparently took the challenge seriously, stating "Oh boy! Jammy Hoffa's, our favorite! Strawberry jelly rolled up in sponge cake . . . with powered sugar on top!"

Neither youngster has been seen since but it is rumored they bought a bus ticket for Chicago.

Reuter's News Service; September 16, 1996

Traffic on the Long Island Expressway was gridlocked for nearly three hours today as motorists were exposed to what was initially thought to be a Jerry Garcia Sighting. A man resembling the recently deceased Grateful Dead band member, was said to be picking up refuse along the side of the road. Reports say that some people actually got out of their vehicles to get a closer look, resulting in congestion that backed traffic up for ten miles.

One witness told reporters that the old man simply vanished into thin air, when a local photographer approached him for a picture.

"It wasn't Garcia, it was an Alien," the witness said. "Who else would pick up trash along this highway . . . no one from this planet."

<u>Author's Notation</u>

The identity and purpose of the Dead Sea Scrolls have eluded scholars for years. Are they really the written history of an ancient people, or simply unsubstantiated blither recorded by local gossip-mongers?

Although the average person has a vague idea about what these historic documents represent, the complexity and controversy keeps most of us in the dark. It is no wonder that when the subject is broached, shoulders shrug and eyebrows rise . . .

Which brings us to the inspiration behind The Mystery of the Dead Squirrels.

I was looking for a new book on The Dead Sea Scrolls for several months after hearing the author speak on a television show. Of course, I had forgotten the title and the author's name so I had nothing to give the bookstore clerk except the subject matter and the fact that it was a new release.

Many weeks went by and there was nothing she could find on her computer or *Books in Print* to confirm that such a book even existed. Finally, after exhausting all possible sources she regrettably informed me she had "checked everywhere, even in the biology section, and there was nothing on the subject of Sea Squirrels, dead OR alive."

The lack of knowledge about these historically enlightening documents is not unique to the bookstore clerk. To prove this point, a random selection of people were asked what they knew about "The Scrolls." The following list made the top ten.

1. messages from God, telling us how to prepare for nuclear war.

2. a rare seaweed that dies when it hits the air.

3. a sailing vessel used by the Jews to cross the Dead Sea.

4. a type-face on a computer

5. a reproductive organ that is no longer functional.

6. a religious document that explains what it is like to be dead.

7. the ornate carvings that decorated the coffins of ancient kings.

8. an herb sold in health food stores, used primarily as a gallbladder cleanse.

9. a trendy new alcoholic drink which is served in a fishbowl.

10. an Indian Tribe that used pregnant women as a sacrifice to the rain god.